Beginner's Mind

EMMA JOAN

Copyright © 2018 Emma Joan
All rights reserved
First Edition

URLink Print and Media
Cheyenne, Wyoming

First originally published by URLink Print and Media. 2018

ISBN 978-1-64367-024-9 (Paperback)
ISBN 978-1-64367-025-6 (Digital)

Printed in the United States of America

Acknowledgments

For the Creator, and this opportunity to allow me to shine my light in his glory...

For my inspirations, Mommy, Grandma Trudy (Emma), Big Sister, Grandma Joan, Uncle Tony, who taught me that no matter how much I learn, I will forever be life's student, if I allow myself to be. Also to live life with humbleness, gratitude, and simultaneously pride. I thank each of them for the amazing, beautiful, encouraging, and wonderful people that they are (were).

For my Angels, Aiyana, Jahsira, Jaleesa, this is for you. You push me to be better every day. You challenge me every day. You force me to keep going and to achieve my dreams so that I can guide you to following yours. I love you!

For my oldest Angel, Kaleb, this too is for you. I hope I am a good example for you to follow, even though there is a lot of distance and age between us. I could not have asked for a better little brother.

For everyone who supported me through this process and this book multiple times and pushed me to be better, thank you so much. I dedicate this book to you as well. You know who you are. Thank you!

Truth Behind Beginner's Mind

Pros and cons extracted. Made known as good and bad.
Reducing knowledge of the wisdom you once possessed,
past tense—had.
Redefining thoughts to figure out where you
left off in your search for understanding
More abrasions to life than conceded, reaching for
pedestals your fingers can't grasp—demanding

Entranced by the fear of not hitting the mark set for one's self.
Dying, but your all you are giving
Suppressed by what you know, what you
can and won't do, oppressed
by the cost of living
Adamant about leading one's own life, no matter what people say
Following the rules of the leader, even if
wrong; one's ways will not sway

Challenging views about facing the real world's animosity,
your thoughts, acting on those thoughts
Being so caught up in one's self, that it is forgotten—
the knowledge taught Half-believing evolution's theory
and half in God's creation of man. Which do I beseech?
So many helpless souls including my own,
so unknowingly, how do I reach?

Chapter One

THE ESSENCE OF JAE

RANDOM THOUGHTS

ABC's

Always
Bout someone
Criticizing my flows
Don't know a thing about me, but for you my words are
Etched in stone
Flipping my words
Got me going insane
Here we are again
I don't even know your name, yet you are
Jumping to conclusions
Kindly step down
Let it be known that you can't touch where my feet tread the ground
Many have tried
None have succeeded, your
Outlook was wrong, wisdom is what you needed
Please stop using my lyrics on a
Quest to make others fear it
Realize true genius is in your own mind
Subject yourself to let your originality flow
Twist your most inner thoughts
You don't need a pen, just strength in thoughts
Vincibility is not the plan

With all of that said and done, your words can take a stand
eXonerate your tone
Yes it will be known, you are where it starts
Zeal cannot be contained when it is over; here is where you yourself can win hearts

Joyful Entry

On May 7, of 84'
God blessed the world and opened heaven's door
To present this angel of a girl
Taking hearts by bundles
Living this so-called life in Detroit's jungles
Giving knowledge to the masses, wisdom she would teach
Ordained by faithful listeners as the worthy and notable PREACH

Findin' Me

It took some soul searchin'
To find what I'm to be learnin', to teach what I don't yet know
Keys to the heart, but where do I go?
Time passes, goals unfurled
Ready for my entry into the real world
Buyin' time
To find
The true me
Truly
Findin' me

Color Scheme

Is it wrong to dig Whites, Arabian Knights?
Those with different eye shades and highlights?
My friends tell me otherwise
Tell me different stories, different lies
Thoughts in my head, I can't place
But everyone thinks that the "safe" place is within the race
Well what is love if it can't cross racial lines?
I'm confused because I should feel liberated, not confined
It puzzles me because my race is all but neither
But words turn my mind into the ultimate deceiver
Slowly but surely becoming a believer
So since I am all and none, can I pick of my inner self and choose a companion?
Why can't it be simple, and not so demanding?
I was always taught that color was a feature, and the real difference is inside...
We think with the same brain, and have the same sense of pride.
So why can't I love outside my race? Allow myself to be deceived by sight?
Would God turn his back on us because of color(s)? It seems,
Than no matter how many races unite, the world is still built on color schemes . . .

Unheard

Silence in the heaviest form
Comin' through calm winds like the heaviest storm
Seen and heard, but not understood
Loving what I say, so I suppose it's all good

How can people say I dig the way, You slay
Words, even nouns, sounds, adverbs,
But I'm speakin' in tongues to you, because you don't understand my words.

Electrical verbs spill from my lips like dribble from a baby
Do I speak mind's references, just words or how I feel? Maybe
Accentuating styles that I use to manipulate phrases and thoughts
Realizing myself that the answer to my mind's question is still sought

Lovin' what I say, but not understanding is like not hearin' me
Writing is what I love, almost like a next of kin, so dear to me
So forgive me if I can't understand how people can't relate to the depth of my words
Heard by the most complex minds, but still unheard . . .

Free Soul

Long lasting, free of pain
Free to gain
All that is laid up to be saved for those worthy of it
Light up my eyes as candles are lit

Free to be myself
Devine intermissions lead me to new faith and wealth
Own decisions, own thoughts, own mind
Truth lies in me to find

Truth found, mission complete-
Not at all times was my soul free
Imprisoned, empty, I left pain just to be
I let pain exist because I knew no more
Nor for what it was in search for

The pain rooted itself deep in my being
The hurt in my eyes showed all I was seeing
But I let go, my pain left like peace
As peace ceased
My pain

I became a whole
Full blown free soul
Opening my new eyes so I could see what was to be
Able to be me . . .

Somehow I Knew

Tangibility—impossible
But your presence is colossal
I sense your heart feeling for my spirit
I feel the treble of your voice even though I can't hear it
I feel your arms and warmth around me protecting and guiding my every step
And even when I do wrong your comfort dwells in me, even while I've slept
When the world turned its back on me and I thought that no one cared,
Somehow I knew you did—'cause you were there
Crying in my pillow, writing on the walls
Walking down familiar, yet unknown halls
The feeling of lonesomeness covered my being
But you opened my eyes to what I should have been seeing
And suddenly, I feel so much better about me
All the while being completed by the Trinity
Everything good has happened because of you,
Even though I couldn't see your face, somehow I knew . . .

My Helpmate

I open the book and it automatically turns to a page
I read what it states—"Until I let go, my heart will be encaged"
I didn't quite understand at first, what this verse meant,
But I knew that somehow, this was a special message sent
I read on and it said to me
In hidden text, "It wasn't meant to be"

I felt my heart drop, because I thought this love would last…
Unfortunately, it became a thing of the past, so fast.
I didn't know that love could be this way
I didn't have time to shed a tear, just time enough to walk away.

I continued to read and the book said, "The right love would soon come to me"
Too much sadness would cause me to stop it, so it would never be
My book also told me, happiness would help me grow,
I now realize that I have to let you go . . .

Through His Eyes

While trying to understand him, I place myself in his position-
Love was missing…

So I look at me . . .

Through his eyes and I see the rain
And with tender applications of love, I remove his pain.
Though tears are still prevalent in his eyes,
I am not allowed to see his lonely cries

But . . .

Through his eyes I see his hopes of the future, plans
Even with the anticipation of heartache, he does what life demands.
Set backs aren't an issue now, he is well on his way
For his goal will be reached, he has come upon his day

Nonetheless . . .

Through his eyes, I see love in its truest form
A love possessing the ability to weather any storm
So tenderly held, it captures me at long last
But the road to eternity is so long—so vast

So dear to me is the fact that . . .

Through his eyes I see him handing me his heart, unbroken—unprepared
I've finally learned to accept it—a love I never dared
So well-hidden are broken promises, that an understanding is posed
That as much as a bridge is between us, our hearts are never closed

But as unfortunate as it may be . . .

Through his eyes I see my hand in his, slowly letting go
I can feel the pain once again in his eyes, but he isn't letting it show.
Just as I disappear forever, I turn for a final glance
Then we both realized that forever came a tad too early, for we never truly gave us a chance . . .

It All Boils Down To

Anger, lust, frustration, hate,
Joy, pain, a strong determination to terminate,
A willingness to give, a need to take
All bets are off at the first sign of heartbreak

Extra tender love convos in the middle of the night
Is it right?
Only the best thing in sight
The thing that makes your soul take flight

Long kisses goodnight, looking deeply into each other's eyes, Hoping that this thing you share will never meets its demise Besides he stares too much and never smiles at you,
And the definition of this thing that should be true is
A devotion of your heart and his

Hoping that you two will never be severed
No matter what the situation, should love expire? Never.
All things may happen, including all things above
If you pay close attention, it all boils down to love.

The Way It Is

"What is it about me?" you ask,
When thoughts of us have long since passed
At last
You come face to face with an unforeseen jolt;
The reality is harsh, but you are strong enough to cope
Unreasonable doubts leave my thoughts to float.
You and me?
Merely a fantasy.
What is it about me that keeps you pressing me?
Everything containing a possibility, and all that you can see,
Should lead you to see, that we this lifetime could not be
Your love has failed to ever express
Pretend you could care less,
And out of no where expect me to fall in love and you don't even call?
Was the plan
To wait until I had a man
And scam your way in?
Let's pretend that I care about your feelings as much as you care about mine.
But trust that this will be a joking matter for years to come, in due time
Your superficial light has faded,
But there is no need to get frustrated,
I know that you hate it
But that's just the way you made it
And that's just the way it is . . .

Emma Joan

Fragrance Flow

Excuse me Mr. Don Juan
I peeped you sexy with your Prada and your Gucci's on
But that's not what caught my attention; it was your fragrance that was so strong,
I've waited so long…
Like Curve and Izzey Miyake
Drakkar Noir and other aphrodisiacs
And your scent had me so I couldn't control my act
It's a fact
That Ralph is giving us a chance
For Romance
And to dance the night away
And I soon become your Obsession
But I must make to you this Confession—
I'm only interested in White Diamonds
And rhymin'
But for now, we can just Be…
Take notice of the air and the slight hue of Chloe'
Happy
Am I as I kiss the wind's lips even though I can't see them
Dig this, I just like the way you smell, I need Freedom…

The Art

Colors matchin' Verbs detachin'
Poetic justice served, but I don't know what I'm lookin' for Heart beatin' fast, head hurtin', but I still want some more Chronic laughter fills my throat as I vibe to your voice
How captivating it sounds as I surrender motion, but not by choice
I think I found the one to make love to my mental
Not just by depth, but completely sentimental
I wish my feelings did not have to be kept confidential
Yet I'm vibin' to your body flow and this instrumental
Totally
You captured me
Made constant sweet memories
Basking in the sunlight with you next to me
Dripping love juice slowly but surely
Completely covering me
Placing me in ecstasy
Lifting my temperature slightly
Dreamin' about your face daily, nightly
Afraid to call you and ask you to vibe with me
Didn't think it was possible to pick up where we L-E-F-T
Off somewhere in my mind, visions of this Unique Soul is complicating my thoughts
And with these thoughts I fought
To gain comprehension
To find the true reason to my heart's ascension and release of tension...

I then realized that it was you
The one with depth perception and a heart so pure and true
My angel of wisdom, shining down on me to allow me to express thoughts without letting them fade...
Even through the blur of tears and life's hazed shade
A true prince was created when God decided on you and your Unique Soul
He knew that your strong spirit would complicate, yet complete me, therefore making me whole
Your eyes had me hypnotized from the very first glance,
And I knew that with this angel I needed every single chance...
So I danced with the option of finding out your style
Trying to comply with things that make you smile,
I tried my hand at investing in love.
Wishing to complete you as you so wanted me to be your spring dove.
I'm in love with your intellect, head over heels with your existence
I'll wait for you forever, because true love requires persistence,
I'm involved in relations on a whole other level, plain, or -x or -y axis,
Physical can't compare to our lyrical climaxes...
Infatuated with your being
You shine like a rare diamond that my love-sick eyes can't help seeing
You are truly beautiful. Sent by God to me -
One of the few who understands the art of "Flowetry"...

360 Story

We made poetry flow right
Our love made rhymes airtight
You by my side, I knew things were alright,
But fatefully our love was vanquished on a humid summer night
Blind becomes my sight as I fight to hold your love's handle
But coldness and pure breeze blow out that candle
Everything I thought I knew,
Turned out not to be true,
Thought we would never bid our love adieu,
But now I bestow this goodbye kiss unto you…
Through -
Finites -
Gone -
A new verse in a similar song
As the one we sang so long ago
And now our poetry don't flow…
So where do we go?
I hear your heart calling, but I unconsciously turn in another direction -
I have immunity against your affection.
Unhappy heart - severed connection …
I can't pretend
To still be in
Love with you

For love, as we call it, is not a feature that is always true
I remember the greatest times…

But at the present, our love makes no airtight rhymes
I can't even touch your heart with a ten foot pole and rubber gloves...
This is not love.
A sharpshooter's beam
Has killed the dream
Of a forever you and I.
And you are probably thinking of any explanation as to why.
I still have not figured it out, but I try with all of my might...
Still hopin' that with you by my side, everything would be alright.
Not tonight-
I type email letters, but my fingers will not press send,
Flippin' through this book of our love, but torn pages I cannot mend -
I'm looking for page one so I can begin,
But the story isn't finished yet, so where do we end?
Tears are fallin' from my eyes, but that just will not do,
Now I am all confused because I miss you . . .

Love (Theory)

Love, I often ask myself what it is. Well, what is love? Love is a test of happiness or heartbreak.
It is one of life's lessons that goes on wild trips and turns through your heart
It pulsates like a raging river; then your sensation is that of drowning.
I've had no real experiences in love before, but I know that it is not worth falling into.
I'm not against love, just the pain of heartbreak that it eventually brings…
Don't get me wrong, I have had love in my life.
But that would have been hard to miss…
Just not the type love that comes unconditionally from a life partner.
It could have been there, and I was never aware…
I know that I am young and may not truly know what love is…
But maybe one day, I'll try it out.

Prisoner of Love

So I fell for you, that was my crime
Here I stand brokenhearted, and I know that it's gonna take some time
For my heart to heal
And I can't continue to feel what I feel
I can't hurt as much as I do
All because I fell in love with you
Why did you ever say that you loved me, knowing it was a lie?
Was your main intention to see if you could make me cry?
If it was, I won't because I am getting so strong.
I have been a prisoner of your love much too long.
Phone calls while I'm with you, now I've became second on your list...
Silly little me, still trying to fulfill your every wish.
Saw that there was a change in scenery, but I paid it no mind
Wasn't looking for anything to incriminate you, but that's all I could find.
If there was someone else, why were you so content in holding on?
When you knew it would hurt me and everything would go wrong.
You knew I was in love with you and I gave you my all.
Still you had the audacity to play me, you wouldn't even call.
I would have done anything for you, I wanted you in my life.
Had illusions of a future with you, and of being your wife...
I guess that love is not all it's cracked up to be, I suppose that for me, it is all wrong.
Cause my heart has been hurting, and I have been a prisoner of your love for far too long...

No Real Answer

All of my life I have searched for the answer to the question of "Why?"
But the answer doesn't come, just the tears of the millions who have cried…
All that is missing is the light of the rising sun.
As the world phases on and the differences are no longer unique,
What becomes the answer to the question, when we know not what we seek?

Promises?...None.

On the day of conception a seed is planted
One that most seem to take for granted—
Most live their lives like they are promised forever, Then it's gone-
When at any time the ropes of life can be completely severed,
Some of us are not even promised the next week, and preparing won't help,
And it seems to make you think you are only hurting yourself
Some of us are not even promised tomorrow and take our last breath in sleep.
Then look from heaven onto what we left, so sorry that we never got a chance not to tell our loved ones not to weep...
But no one can truly know the end, because the hour is unknown,
When your life may come to an end, and your body will no longer be your home.

IKnowNow

Dimensional dissention from where I once was
Confused because I thought I found this thing called love
- Called love
I steadily searched to find - I
Wanted so much for it to be mine - I
Watched it slip from my grasp as - I
Cried tears as my love died...

Never Been

New experiences as I age
New love blossoms, but still I feel this empty space.
I've felt love, pain, and the hurt of loss and the joy of gain
I've been caressed, finessed, the object of one's affection...
But I have never been a first love
I've traveled, been dazzled by things that I have seen...
I've loved, been loved, been hated
But of all the people that I have met, no one could have ever related
To the only one in the world to have never been a first love
Perhaps it's my fate
Or maybe, just maybe I was always too late
Picking up pieces of shattered hearts, but never the one to break...
And for some reason I feel as though my heart is going to burst
As I secretly wonder if someone out there has the same feelings for me that I had for my first . . .

Wonder..Land

By and by time goes as I search for my call...
It seems that everything that I search to pursue turns into a brick wall
I break barriers to get to my destined place
But hunger fills my soul as I long for just a taste
The green in my eyes searches for the pot of dough
At the end of the rainbow
Time is ticking and slowly diminishing my plan
As I rapidly descend to the ground I wonder ... Where will I land?

Platinum Visa

Passport to hidden lands
Dark and light sands
Combine to make hands
Feet
Mouths that speak, yes greet
Me
Oceans roar and splash against rocks looking for a spot to land
Odd how it demands
Space
To grace
The sandy beaches
Most comfortable spot into hidden pleasures
Finding ways to uncover buried treasures
The sun beams down looking for shadows to disintegrate
Old to rejuvenate, young to reinvigorate
Trees line the south beach taking it under shade's wing
To bring
Cool comfort to those sun-dressed
Who want fun, nonetheless
Magnificent night skies rise, showing the stars ablaze in the atmosphere…
Most fear
The night sky
Making futile attempts to make the stars cry
The love of the seas teases us,
Pleases us…
And this can all be yours with a platinum visa

All in My Head

Thoughts of anguish cross my mind...
Horrid unsightly nightmares cause my heart to become blind.
Shattered dreams filled with despair,
And it seems as though no one in the world could possibly care.
Expressions of sadness plague my inner being,
I don't know if seeing is believing or if believing is seeing...
Challenges endured...
But my future is still not secured,
Sometimes understanding life is just so hard
I must go along with the dealer and just "Pick a card"
I wish I knew the difficulties of all that lies ahead, or the answer to every question said...
Maybe one day I will see that it's all in my head.

I Know

I know he doesn't want me, but I don't let it show,
Every time he lies and tells me that he loves me, lmy feelings for him grow...
Yet, whenever I talk to him, it seems I always cry;
And it seems that he wishes that I wouldn't try
- Or have dreams for us
- Because he holds this thing dear to him called temporary lust

I know I shouldn't think about him so much,
- Or even let my heart peak from his touch
- But the truth of the matter is, when he holds me, I clutch
My frowns turn to smiles when he comes into view
My only hope is that he will one day feel what he says is true

How can love be so wrong?
And have me feeling so sprung?
How could it have made me so blind to see?
That everything was so wrong for me?

For You

I would cross the ocean a millions times if it would make your heart content,
I would write your name in the heavens above to show you exactly what I meant
I would become a genie to fulfill your every wish and make you smile at me
I would endure the hardest task possible so that you could see
For you, my heart beats a hundred times a minute
For its sheer excitement that you are in it...
My feelings for you grow every time I think about you, see you, touch you, kiss you,
And when we are apart, you just don't know how much I miss you
You just don't know how much joy I feel when you hold me so tight,
Just being in your arms, I know that everything will be alright
I want to be able to do that for you
Because your love is the simplest form of heaven—so divine, so true...

Anew

As I stare at you sleeping so beautifully,
I see heaven in my mind's eye...
More precious than any gift ever given to me
I have received you, my beautiful angel in disguise.
I see an eternity of love that we will make worth living,
A love to weather any storm
For you I give, and will never stop giving
I promise to love you with not only my heart, but my spiritual form
Now I know this feeling is deep,
When I see a life without you, I begin to weep
For I love you so much
As I stare at you sleeping so beautifully
I can't help but wonder why
The spell you put upon my heart,
I know will never die
Now I will never question fate
For I feel your love inside
I have finally found my soul mate
No longer must I hurt, try, or cry . . .

My Angel

Just as I was giving up on love,
I was sent this angel from above.
To touch my heart and bring my smile.
With a kiss to make past pain worthwhile.
He touched my soul as a confidant and friend,
And slowly, surely my heartache he began to mend.
He held me close and wiped away my tears,
And as my protecting angel, he removed my fears
I still do not understand why I have received such beauty and perfection,
Or why this angel made me his only selection.
I can only be thankful for my serenity and peace
For everyday is now a sunny day, and my dark clouds have ceased.
I can never thank him for his infinite love
But only be grateful—he is my own personal, perfect angel from above...

Emma Joan

Not Enough... (For Willie Mae)

Thinking... thinking so hard on what to say for a few too many nights....
What words could I use to illuminate a light that was already so bright?
How do you describe the inner and outer beauty of a rose, when its sight needs no description?
How do you put into words the way that you feel, when you know that words could never be that descriptive?
"I miss you" doesn't seem fitting, but it's all I can think of at the moment... "I love you" also seems like it wouldn't be enough, but it's all that I can go with...
"I wish I had more time with you" opens the door a little more, and gives a good place to start,
But "I need you here and now forever", even though it's not possible, is what's really in my heart.
Forever.... It's an odd word. And even though I know it's not possible, I know that I have said it infinite times, believing that it would always be,
Believing that I would never be standing here with you there and these words coming from me...
Wishing that you could just tell me one more time that it doesn't matter what happens, that God has a plan,
And that I may not understand it, but it's for his glory, not that of man.
And I wish that me wishing you here would bring you back, because we need you so much...
If not for a word, or a listening ear, then for a sweet smile, big hug, or gentle touch.

And for our heavy hearts, feeling that it is too hard to move past today, I know we, at some point, will hear your voice inside telling us "Do it anyway.
And in doing so, be better than you ever thought possible to be, And do it to the Glory of God and in remembrance of me".
You may not be here where we can see you, but you will never be hard to find
Because you will always be with us, keeping you close in heart and in mind.
Love you always...

Love Pretense

And the survey says: She's evading love.
Why? Because it hurts too much- it's not supposed to hurt
But it feels so good, even when its wrong-
How can love be wrong? Initiation under
inconspicuous pretenses, but
endured nevertheless.
And the survey says: She's been burned by love.
How so and in such good spirits? Because,
love intentionally hurts and is
only out for its happiness- not that of
either party involved in its devious
and Machiavellian ploys.
Yet interestingly enough she is willing to try it again, and again—
Until all the toads turn into prince charmings . . .
But honestly, if she loves and she can't
get love to go away when love is
supposed to be over, how can she ever get away from it?
And the survey says: She's confused, because she still loves . . .

Chapter Two

TO YOU

PREACH'S SOUL STORIES

Sweet

Untouched, untapped
So pure, unwrapped
We love as close as two hearts can
As I no longer run from - and embrace - like a baby learning to stand
We vibe out a melody
And you think as I do- so close to me
H-A-R-M-O-N-Y
Melodious love tunes
Swoon
My mind
As I find
Love, true this time

Spellbound

When I first met you, I had this flicker of desire. Not quite a flame or a fire, just desire
Could have been lustful momentary infatuation-but that wouldn't last long
Though it was neither right nor wrong
It was somewhere in-between...

What could it possibly mean?
Am I never to understand as this-this thing grows?
Into more, It becomes what I am looking for.
But it is neither here nor there.
A feeling like this in my time is now rare
So what am I to expect from this gentle soul so exquisite, so right?
Containing the ability to block all others from my sight?

From a different universe in a parallel world, he plucks stars from the sky for me in his song
But it is neither right nor wrong, But somewhere in-between

But what is to happen if others intervene? What could possibly become of this?
What would begin or end if I attempt to touch his lips?

Dream To...

To dream - to verify anything not reality
To escape into a world of pure and just thought - sometimes
Sometimes as the wind whispers past my ear
I turn to see where it has gone

It may have turned into absolutely nothing or helped to develop a storm
It's not real, but it feels stronger than the presence of life
Emotions deep, deep, deeper, feels to good to be true
Just like a ... dream

Sometimes serene, sometimes nightmarish
To bear it is almost impossible, possible to feel
Impossible to rid yourself of
Dark clouds in a morbidly light sky

Pass away to dark skies
And forever a cloud stands, too bright not to notice, too dark to get rid of
A blemish in heaven's perfect setting
How can it be unreal?

Uplifting tones liberate life as time stops...
Life, byproducts of dreams, dreams, byproducts of life.
Twists, turns, uncontrollable spinouts, ice storms, long, narrow winding roads ...
To dream, to verify anything not reality
To escape into a world of pure and just thoughts

Sometimes ...

The Question

As I try to find the answer, I search within your eyes. As I sit with you, all I can do is deny
How I feel for you, Though all I feel is true, It is beyond too late.
Without your love, I must continue, herein lies my fate
My mind concentrates on hopes that you will ask
But the truth remains that I took too long, and that moment has since passed…
As we sit silently, I wonder what wanders in your mind,
With a hope that this momentary visitation isn't all that we find.
I have a confession-
If our love was as strong as we supposed, where lies the question?

Call

Can't stop thinking about you
Even if I tried.
I remember my girl asked if I was diggin' you, I said no, I lied.
So when I searched my soul for the answer as to why you were not here,
It was obviously because of the miscommunication of our hearts was all uncertain, yet clear.
So I ponder the choices I have made and the thoughts that I think of you
And the feelings that I hold dear to me, so far away, yet so true.
How could I think of your kisses, when none have even graced my cheek?
Or the warm embrace of your oh, so tender arms that I imagine would have my knees weak...
Or the scent of you that pleased my every single sense,
Or the way that you said my name; a way I've longed to hear it ever since.
How could I just let you be without saying how I feel at all?
Or pretend that you are just my buddy, when you call?
If I could get up close and personal, I swear I would risk it all
But at the present time, I sit here waiting, til I get that call . . .

I Tried (Letter to My Heart)

First off, I must apologize for the pain that I caused you
I know that you think I have broken my promise, but to you I am still true.
You have to give me one more chance and let me try love again,
If it doesn't work, we will never do this again and you win.

Right now, I feel like I can handle it and it won't hurt too much,
But the more it hurts, the better it feels, and I am addicted to his touch…
My mind is telling me to do it, but you are telling me no
Please, just let me try love, just one more time, then I promise I'll let go

I'll try not to break you again, but no promises will I make,
If you hurt again, it's a part of life, and it's a risk we will just have to take.
Now if I fall again, don't be afraid, or even think I lied,
No one could ever stay away from love, but at least I tried…

Orchestra Love

Deep cellos
Whisper soft and sweet hellos…
Hellos; 1-2-3-4 count-half rest
Basses, heartbeats, deep breaths…
Violins sing restlessly of a love no longer
Rest-rest; how as being destroyed had gotten stronger

Arpeggio hearts skip a beat for a whole note; 1-2-3-4
The music crescendos as my heart hits the floor
Boom goes the bass drum, the beat slows down
D-O-W-N slows down the tempo as the violins are drowned
Out by the cellos melody
The first chair spot provides a vacancy…

Repeat before 1st rest - deep cellos and their soft and sweet hellos…
Rest-rest; violins prepared for a solo
Rest-rest; playing so soft in moderation, so low - unheard
Drowned out by the bass one more time the violin rests;
1-2-3-4
And again the music crescendos as my heart hits the floor…

It's OK

Precariously, I stumble upon humble thoughts, thoughts unworthy of thinking
Minds subject to change in one's eye blinking Comfort zones left for appropriate reasons indeed Words spoken from a heart that doesn't bleed

It's ok that an unbeatable heart lies bleeding
Losing life not aware of what it is needing

Occupying thoughts that shouldn't be entertained
Where go, these thoughts show feelings that shouldn't be there
Is it the intensity of the convos or his soft curly hair?

It's ok that I love you, yet haven't the slightest clue as to why
Can't possibly fathom these feelings though I try

I must say this is a growing experience, I have learned a lot from you
But mostly I understand now that to myself I must be true
I feel as though time is telling me to wait
But fear of being alone tells me it's far too late

It's ok that my heart cries out to you in the middle of the night
Purposely wishing you were there to make it right
But don't worry, my sorrows won't stay
My pain will be over soon, it's ok.

Should I

Should I believe in happiness or anything thereof?
Should I remember anything that you taught me about how to love?
The same love that was so soon betrayed
When we laid
A foundation for life that would last forever

You told me that there was nothing to worry about
That the candle of our love would never be blown out
But as love fools me again, I realize
That everything you said to me was the pretty part of a fantastic lie

Should I believe that I could have ever loved you more?
Given all the pain you had in store
Should I believe that my heart can mend?
Should I ever be foolish enough to love again?
Should I just block my heart from ever loving at all?
Should I close my ears whenever love calls?
Will all love be as it was with you?
How could something that's supposed to be so beautiful, be so untrue?

And If I Did . . .

Revelation to me
That eyes do not always show what's in front of me
Some things are not meant to see
Until it's too late
Seeming loveless as my fate

No problem with finding love have I
Just the intensity of pain when it is gone lingers in my eyes
And what if I did turn my back on love and all the pain that it brings
Now free of love, not enduring hurt, rejoicing fully, my heart sings

So many times love has proved to me that it goes far from gain
But the loss of it potentially blinds me, forcing me to go insane
Curse the dawn that love fell upon me, missioning to break my heart
I didn't know its intentions, and now without further thought, I know I want no part

So what if I turn my back on love, its happiness hit me hard
But the temporary high soon went away, now I am permanently scarred
I was so sad that it had ever existed
Still, most tell me that it is better to love, than to ever have missed it

Dream Alone Tonight

My world crumbles and crinkles,
Crumbles and wrinkles,
Around me all I see is an empty vastness
Complete and utter void
Not like I am checking my back, but I've become newly paranoid.

Destroyed is my spirit- they are bringing me down
Don't show it, but the love I need cannot be found
Silence is sound
I miss what I have longed for that I finally come to grips
My soul has been ripped- from me

And I wish for tranquility
I know the will is in me
But my vision blurs my sight so suddenly
What has become of me?

No longer fully functioning
I move as dead weight
But I constantly rush fate -
No one can relate

It doesn't phase me
From what those around me see
I embrace my strength constantly
Not just for the I, but We
I continue leading blindly, yet still sheltered from harm
And as we dream our dreams alone, I see you right back here in my arms...

Hopeless Thoughts

If I could only . . .
To get only part of what I give
Then I wouldn't be lonely
And have more happiness in this life I live
Timeless moments with my one and only

If I could only . . .
To give my love to a worthy heart
My fears may have ceased
And revitalized every part
Just as long as my thoughts have peace

If I could only . . .
To hold his hand in mine
With a thought of a kinder existence
And a delightful touch of his lips,
But should I try to resist this?

If I could only . . .
To know the truth just one time
And I will need to know no more
And give my poem a bit of rhyme
And I can continue searching for what I am looking for

If I could only . . .
Say what I think and not be repetitive or redundant
Find that the truth may hurt, but I will still live
And without it, it seems
That I run through a field of hopeless dreams
Hopeless thoughts I think while I imagine what I would do . . .
If I could only . . .

Realizing

Tender love songs
Play as our love goes wrong
Heartbroken I stand
And a single hairline strand
Of our love falls to the floor
How could I be in a position
And didn't know what was missing
What you needed was so much more…
Another road taken
Hearts, minds, bodies and souls forsaken
And I try not to cry
Bonded souls separate, losing sight
As pain takes flight
Thus comes the end of you and I

Another Turn

Thought that without you I could not go on
But it seems that as in so many situations, I was wrong
How long can we go on with this charade and pretend?
We both know the love isn't there anymore, so is this where we end?

I shouldn't say that the love isn't there anymore, for I love you still
I speak of what I see and you show what you feel
You didn't make a mistake in letting go
If you were staying for my benefit, thanks but please let go

You say that you want to be with me, and forever, us to be true
But you hurt me with your words, and I can see that I am hurting you
Maybe you were right, and we weren't meant to be
I made you feel terrible and you did the same to me

Let's not say our love was wasted, instead it's a lesson well learned
As much as I would love to stay, I can't make another turn

Different

Once I knew you, I was captivated by your charm
I loved your smile, the way you held me in your arms
I knew your heart

Once I knew the wisdom you possessed inside
The way your speech was so eloquent, the was you carried yourself with pride
I knew your worth

Once I knew the love you had for me and how I made you feel
The way you proved your heart to me and showed me that our love was real
I knew your depth

Once I knew passions, the goals you had for the future
You had unlimited potential and you were my perfect suitor
I knew your ambitions

But somehow your views have changed in ways I never would have believed,
And as you send the revised you across, you transmission may not be received
I know not this person standing in-front of me
Was he always there and you were make believe?

Still Doesn't Make Sense

The question he poses
As the gap in his arms closes
Around me
Is "What do you see?"
I look closely into his eyes
And try to deny
What I visualize so vividly
He and me
Lovely
He smiles at me because he sees my thoughts...
I am caught
In his illustrious fantasy
Where it is only we
Engaging in kisses so extraordinary
Where I become trapped in love's holding
Love's molding
No less than amazing
Is his soft hand
Beckoning for more time, so that we can follow his plan
Standing and demanding that I show him my inner being
Not believing
That my complications won't excite him

I had to make him understand that love isn't forced, just posed upon a thought provoked whim...
And as I turn and walk away
I realize that it didn't make sense for me not to stay
But it was too late...

How It Should Be . . .

Listen
My heart stopped beating because your love was missing
Just holding your hand or the way your eyes glisten
The mistake was made, but pride won't let us reconcile for the sake of you and I
I invent ways to try to forget your name
It's a shame
That when I can't remember my own
Yours becomes my mental throne
But we are done
And you are gone—
One try wouldn't last it
Two tries haven't passed it
And you should keep trying
'Cause I won't stop our love from dieing . . . but
I want its life to be everlasting that one thing that you can look at, and know that t will always be there
That thought in the back f your head that says I will always care
And though we are not together, you still hold the key to my heart
And our love will live long after us, and our hearts will never part

If We Label This . . .

What we have is good Better than it ever should Be- better than love Above

Everything it should be
Could it be that we
Share something more than a friendship?
More than sweet kisses on the lips?

But if we label this . . .
We could lose everything that we would possibly miss
Maybe it's more than just physical attraction
Maybe it's that "1-4-3" and we need to take action

But let's silence the maybes as we engage in a kiss
Cause if we label this . . .
We could lose it all in new moments of bliss
We would be taking unnecessary risks
So . . . We should leave it as is
Continue in our ways of admiration
Not to become love or dedication
So let's enjoy this kiss . . .

Don't let go of what we have, let's not label this . . .

Gimme That

Genes strong enough to make me wonder about the background -
Thoughts about the things he says in my mind going round Countenance that of an angel
Words and actions to bring him down, he mangles.
Height of intellectual capacity higher than any ever known
The beauty of it is that he isn't even fully grown
Did I mention that his conversation is so wise that is captures and perplexes me
Tempo of his speech vexes me

I say—Gimme that -

Speaking his mind
A jewel like this, I've been searching to find
Opening doors, pulling out chairs, I didn't know that they still made men like this
The part that I dig the most is . . .
His mental impressions are flawless, with positive effects that last
Because his Mother raised him with class
Now picture that . . . .

True

The earth turns faster, people continue pressin' And I'm confessin'
That when I'm with you, I see nothing but you
It's true -

My world stops as the vastness about me goes on at a continuous pace,
Is it really my place
To love you?
Only God and moms above you?
You gotta be right for me—gotta be -
Got me feelin' lovely

Can't wait til it can just B-E
Y-O-U and M-E ... Reality hits me
I can't control my love for you, but in due time
We will flow right; for now, we just rhyme

Thinkin' that our pace accelerates with each moment that will pass
Holdin' each other like each moment is our last
Still can't help but feel that we are moving too fast ...
Glad that sex is not a factor in this love that we make,
Time we take

My best friend-
And with you next to me, I win again and again
Mentally love me
I can feel your presence even when you are not with me
Continuously my heart you abscond

And it's so natural the way we bond
And ooh, when we kiss so tenderly, so peacefully
I become you, you and I become we
Slowly—
As the earth turns faster and people continue pressin'
I'm confessin' that when I'm with you, I see nothing but you—
It's true . . .

Regrets

I'm looking at the clock searching for time...
Wondering why life no longer has rhyme -
Or reason

Inside traitors possess the knowledge and the will for treason
And the death toll quickly rises as we change season
Tick-tock

Time is slowly ticking into an abyss
Who ever would have thought it would be like this?
External as well as internal war is waged
A cowardly leader's position is staged

Maybe it is just a phase and I am way too concerned Funny how our "Leaders" do nothing as cities are burned Lives are turned
In sorrowful directions
People having doubts about who was chosen in the last election

Oddly enough, most knew war was coming at his right-hand side
And he knew nothing of his position and took a country of naïve believers along for the ride
Pride
Anchors him and he won't step down
Even if his drunken decisions cause the destruction of everyone around,
look around -

A peaceful nation has turned to turmoil and confusion Families are weakened and torn apart—still no solution These times are some that the world will never forget
As happy smiles have turned into a cries, a nation mourns, sighs, - regrets...

Separation

Rural American cities
Drastically overtaken Makin'
Solutions
Conclusions
About how good they got it -
The nation's equation
Is separation
Of church and state
How long must I wait
For devastation to take over
For the world to get colder?
Holding boulders on my shoulders
'Cause life has become bolder
Showing that it's not afraid of death, life, living
Just breaking down and giving
Corruption at every angle
Hearts and bodies mangle
From the tangle
Of community devices -
Everyone is so quick to tell you what your life is . . .
The nation's equation
Is separation
Of mom and dad

Forgot the values that family once had
Now an extinct entity and the products of no morals is me -
To grow a life lacking the knowledge of man, just understanding woman
Can a man
Do whatever he plans?
Do I stand
Idly by and let advantage be taken of me?
If. I learned one thing from dad; it's not to accept what they told me I had to be.
The nation's equation
Is separation
Of black and white
Remember first left then right
Years have passed and the situation
Is still about racial denomination
Dividing our nation
Still creating agitation
Frustration
Yet determination
But nontheless, separation ...
The nation's equation
Is separation
Of poor and rich
Got middle class folks believin' life's a bitch
"Cause our tax dollars go to Inauguration Balls
Long distance Presidential Calls
But what can you give me when I trip and fall?
The tricks of the trade make the rich get richer and the poor get poorer

And no matter how much we don't have, you still take more
The nation's equation
Is neglect of a nation
Frustration
Yet determination
But still separation...

Mental Block/Depth Perception

Most legendary thoughts equipping the mind
With knowledge of the past, but what is there to find?
I look deep inside myself, searching for internal wealth
But depth is not a feature, time must be my teacher
Depending too much on things that don't much matter
Bubbles cover my body as the soap lathers
Thoughts become complicated and unsure
Cloudy minds are too rarely endured
How can mysteries plague the way I think and they don't even pertain to me?
I dig a little deeper to find all of the answers untold
Like how I can be so warm in a world so cold?
Does one who attempts to manipulate someone's mind manipulate his own?
Am I trying to get you to think like me?
Growing hearts of stone in a field
I yield crops
To try to bridge the generational gap
Gain the knowledge I lack
And take back what I should own
Depth isn't a feature
Gotta learn that if I got a hard head, time must be my teacher, preacher, life source and source of remorse.

Not Alone

One set of footprints in the cement after it was solidified
I placed them there and since then I have cried
A heavier weight than I could have ever imagined, thrown at the depth of my existence…
As soul, body, mind and heart push hard on this great resistance
As I concentrate and fall, I realize the extent of my life's work…
I realize that most that I have endured, didn't hurt…
I strive with a strength that I've never known….
Because it didn't come from me; into his spirit I have grown
My hands have done no works they were just a vessel, a tool for him to use
When I completed tasks that I would have never passed, because I had no clue.
My burdens seem lighter, I barely feel them as I travel throughout the day
And I smile up above 'cause it's all love and he came to make my way
Now I feel like I'm floating and I understand why there was only one set of footprints in the cement after it was solidified
Because he carried me, my troubles too, and those were his tears that I cried.

Even Though—I Was Still In Love . . .

So he's got me,
And no one could have stopped me
I tried not to be temped by his sexy eyes and soft skin
Exquisite features not possessed by other men

Or the way he made love like he did it for TV -
And said that it was just for me -
I knew there were others sharing my wealth
But I couldn't think of those, just moments that I had him to myself

But so many continuously intruded and occupied his time -
A time which I thought was all mine -
But forsaken and undertaken by an undeniable charm
I couldn't understand how such a lovely creature could do my heart so wrong

Even though I was still in love
He told me not to feel for him, but I have become so accustomed to his touch
And if you could feel it too, you would see why I love it so much.
So many have fallen victim to his smile and kisses
And I can't blame them, for when he is gone, I too shall miss this -

He has captured so many hearts including my own
But I can't fight to the finish for his heart's throne
But it's cool I suppose, because I fell, and all else above
Even though, I admit it, I was still in love

He had my nose wide open and my eyes wide shut - I would have done anything for this boy
Hence, the feeling was not mutual, and I was but a mere toy
Still I let him engulf me, make love to my mental
But as he walks away, I see so clearly that these feelings were accidental -

I should have listened to myself; I could have hurt me no more
Than the one that crushed my heart, the one that I adore
I probably shouldn't have wanted him and all else above,
I probably shouldn't admit it, but I was in love . . .

Chapter Three

THE REST OF ME

OUTRO MEETING EMMA JOAN

Love Is . . .

Love is to be long and received living
Love is to be in a constant state of giving
Love is to be given in doses of a million cups a day
Love is never worried about others getting in the way
Love is always in a constant state of bliss
Love can be transferred by one touch of the other's lips
Love never lets go of its heart's true desire
Love doesn't let go of its heart, no matter what may transpire
Love is known for never angering from not receiving what it wants
Love is known for thinking of everyone else before self, and never flaunts
Love wants love as much as anyone could ever know
But love isn't really love, because it always lets go . . .

Fallen Love

Slowly fading, but not yet gone;
Short weakened breaths, but my heart is still strong.
I am not looking forward to seeing the great light
But oddly, making dances with the night
Slow dances with the wind with not yet a love lost,
But events from the past made my heart the cost.
Everlasting and eternal the fire did burn
Over time, my trust it did earn…
Love was forced upon us by the undying sun
Love forced upon us did force us to become one
Acts of lust pushed us apart -
And again the cost was my heart
Let a rose pressed by time wither in its lonely sandcastle alone
The petals begin to fall one at a time, slowly descending its throne…
No longer queen, destined for death at the beginning
But remembered as wonderful and never-ending
Never to be forgotten, for it truly was the best
Lying preserved and undead upon eternal rest

And They Say...

And they say that it is better to love than to have not loved at all ...
Unless love becomes the source of all gone wrong ...
And they say that when it's real it always comes back home ... So wish on star upon star til your love is no longer gone ...

And they say that as many times as you hurt each other you can always try again ...
And whatever you start in the process of pain, eventually floats on with the wind ...

And they say that love is rambunctious and impossible to tame ... But when put to the test, all in all, actions prove truth in its name ...

And they say that the makings of love are born in simple moments of pleasure ...
And when it is meant, nothing can stop it from lasting forever ...

Explain What You Can't understand

Explain—my love for you runs, can you catch it?
Deeper than the ocean...
It's far greater than any planet
Cannot be touched or severed by any other emotion

Explain—temptation and lust fill me
Why you and not my own? Discovering thoughts found now
Or can it wait until I am grown?

Explain—engulfed in passion—that would otherwise not be there
Temperatures rise at every motion
Ecstasy brought to mind with single connotations
Your every move becomes my most forbidden notion

Explain—fantasizing melodic tunes playing—exotic trees swaying
Walking hand in hand on a sandy beach
Suns set, then rise, right before our eyes
So close, yet not within our reach

Explain—but I can't ... it is not possible to explain what one cannot understand
Temptation, lust, love, attraction, the simplest way
Cannot explain a vibe of any sort
Or trust thoughts or emotions that should not stay...

Untouchable Dream

Walks hand and hand in the park
Staring at the moon long after dark
Drinking a Sprite at the same time, from the same cup
And my heart skips a beat every time I look up
My love, endless love, the only one for me;
I mean -
Now I realize that I am reaching for the untouchable dream

Nights spent cuddling, looking into each other's eyes,
Sitting on sandy beaches, watching the sun rise,
Soft forehead kisses and gentle back rubs,
Candlelit dinners and rose-petal filled tubs,
Dancing the night away, fortunate to be together, Promising to be together forever.
It's so odd, yet beautiful it seems,
And still I sit here dazed, reaching for the untouchable dream

Holding each other close, talking by the fireside
Or going out for a night on the town, just to ride
Gazing into each other's eyes, or mouthing "I love you" from across a table
To see you and do anything; I feel able.
Wrapping your arms around me, or kissing me on my neck's nape
So whatever happens when a dream defers, and reality takes shape?

Blinded by this thing called love, not believing what's true,
Like looking into the sky and saying it's any other color than blue
The most beautiful experience my life has ever seen -
Too bad it wasn't real, maybe one day there will be hope for the untouchable dream . . .

Love? Not Love

He looks me in my eyes, kisses my lips, Caresses my cheek, calmly kisses my hand, He holds my heart, refusing to let go,
But I hold nothing of his but a physical glow.
"Understand" he tells me, "that we are in a crucial moment in time,
Emotions will grow eventually, and I dig your heart and mind",
Yet I feel the emptiness when he wanted me to love him
Now I do and I have nothing to show
But what do I know?
Perhaps I know nothing, am intrigued by his bright smile, and dimpled eyes
His soft features, goofy laugh or great hugs -
I realize it is just enjoyment and like—not love . . .

By and Bye

By the things that I have to think, because he won't say...
By the things I have to miss, because I'm not sure if he will stay,
By the look in his eye, because he knows I want more,
Because he constantly pounds my heart into the floor.
By the way I can't love him anymore because it hurts so much...
By the distant body, that trembles from his vacant touch,
By the way he doesn't know that he hurts me so bad;
Because he is still a child and family is all that he had.
By the way she hurt him, and now I have to deal,
By the way I can't show love, because I don't know if his is real,
By the lack of emotion, for everything pertaining to me;
Because he needs something I don't have, so desperately.
By the way I don't know him, the way I thought I did,
By the way he keeps his feelings so perfectly hid,
By the way, he makes me feel that he just settled, because he was tired of running around...
Because for months I haven't even been able to make him smile.
By the way that I'm exhausted, so tired, tired of trying,
By the way I have to stop and say goodbye, but it won't stop my heart from crying...

How Would You Feel?

Suppose I did the things that you do, how should I expect you to feel? Or maybe if I made plans with other men, what would be your first idea? Or if I looked at dudes on T.V. like you could never compare,
How would you feel if I did it to you while you were sitting there? Would you love me the same, if when I went out of town
And you constantly had to wonder what was going down?
Or if I had things in my past that stayed "situations" when they should be done,
Would you still see me as the perfect prize that you had won?
Could I honestly ignore your feelings and act as though you don't exist - Without you calling me evil, hateful or even selfish?
Could I look at you and lie with no remorse at all,
And tell you that I love you with no intent at all?
Could I say that I was thinking about you, when I'm really thinking of someone else?
And tell you that I love you, just when I want something for myself?
Could I intentionally hurt you constantly and not be real?
If I did all of this to you, tell me, how would you feel?

Loveless

How do you love a loveless heart, full of void and potentially incapable of love?
With no hope of a returned feeling, pressing on for and inkling of intent
To love -
But lifelessly love less ...

How do you love a loveless heart that speaks ill of those that love too much?
Not noticing that you too are categorized with those possessing such love
But while being processed, are hindered from existence
How do you love a loveless heart?

Without attempting to hate love, you become its loveless counterpart
Engaging in this feeling drifting, drifting into an abyss of love, but still interacting with the world as loveless-
To mend a loveless heart is not an option, for you must become that which is to conquer it
But if it is not to be conquered, then it is just to be
Perhaps this loveless heart is just not ready for love
Or maybe this loveless heart has been hurt by love and refuses to love again -
How, if possible, do you love a loveless heart?
One cannot tell of such a feat that has been completed with success

Yet and still ... I try ...

Say Goodbye

As I walk away, I wonder,
Has my decision caused a blunder?
A decision to get back on track with my goals and my life
To be a good friend, never mind a wife
This wasn't my plan; I never meant to make you cry,
And the thought of hurting you, made me not even want to try...
But I realize that I made a decision that would affect two hearts
And I can no longer handle the strain, we must part.
As time goes on, we see a new lesson in the mold
"Just cause" isn't enough reason and it makes hearts grow cold
It is time to say goodbye and completely let me go
For I have completely let go of you and given myself room to grow...

Who's At Fault?

"Are you blaming the right one?" I ask as my heart hardens.
I'm not guilty, yet I feel it necessary to be pardoned.
You left me wondering about the future when it was right within your grasp;
You play countless games and wonder how when I see you, I pass.
Yesterday didn't last forever and it sure isn't today,
So why do you go out of your way
To make me feel as though I have so much to lose?
When you are to blame, you made me choose -
You had your chance; don't be mad that it is gone
I waited for you, ever so patiently; so long
But now that I have moved on,
In your eyes, I can't help but be wrong
Now there's a "him" and he gives my heart a sense of protection,
And I find it incredible that I don't have to fight for his affection
You let me go without a second thought -
So the question that has already been answered is
Who is really at fault?

Undecided

Walking toward the door, but I can't decide what to do. Don't feel like all is lost, 'cause I still love you
But the way I feel right now just is not right,
So it's time for us—our love to say goodnight
Sleep toward dreams of a perfect relationship—perhaps not even for us
One of pure love, honesty and trust—no lust
I want to be with you, but that's something I can't allow
The route we are going, it's impossible to even fathom how
For a while, the love had been fading, and now it's gone;
Don't you remember when it was so strong?
Perfect harmony we sang under an endless moonlit sky
As far as the eye could see, forever you and I
Things have changed since we have been together – and I don't exactly know what went wrong
I guess there's no need to second guess myself. Maybe it's time to say goodbye, to our love - so long . . .

Through It

Going through some things
So I turn my head to the sky
I wish I could grow wings and fly
How much can I bear?
God please let me know
I know that you are there
But this trying thing stunts my spiritual growth
My master account is all out of dough
And I've got nowhere to go
I know I can bear it some and you will never put more on me than I can,
But who would have ever thought that my heaviest burden would be a man?

Glance At Past Mistakes

When he walks past me
And his eyes are all I see

Vaguely I drift into his sight
And as innocent as I might Have been
When his touch became my sin

Should I have never partaken in such sheer delight
As many delectable nights?
In the presence of one which I thought would last forever
Maturity, spirituality and desire

All that he had, simultaneously lacked; to snuff out the flames of a dying fire
And as time grew, so did we and our connections has long since been severed
But at the thought of him, I might have smiled or smirked
For had it not been for growth, it might have worked . . .

Love Defined

I've been told by someone who knows
Exactly how love flows,
By experience how it goes
How as you age, the more it shows
More than before
The words spoken to my time sensitive mind, told me that the love I felt could not be...
That it was merely chemistry—CHEMISTRY...
Magnetism, attraction in its most complex form
And if it could overpower love's storm
Then it was love—a step higher than this
More than a thought, wish, or kiss
More than chemistry that could just be lust or bliss
Not words, only actions that cannot be undermined,
Then will one truly be able to experience something truly worthy of love, defined...

I Hear You

Weakness comes over me; How can this be?
Speaking of love juice and sundress explorations;
You are saying a lot, but what is your final destination?
I see your eyes glowing, deep brown; where do I begin?
I hear a sweet and mellow voice saying, "When can we vibe again?"
Whenever you can, I can -
But you need a moment of my time, you say
Anything to make me come your way . . .
I call you up and we speak in rhyme
And no one understands how we can call this a good time.
I picture my side at your side,
Your glide with my glide,
Hand in hand,
You tell me that we vibe so well, you want to take the place of my man
I hear you talking, but don't get angry if I don't buy
And if I avoid what you say, that doesn't mean don't try
How 'bout you show me more than words—your words are nice
But what's left to say after you insist that hundreds of our closest will be throwing rice?
Your flow is on top, but it is all in what you do;
So don't get mad if all I say is "I hear you" . . .

R U Thinkin' Bout Me?

R u thinkin' bout me?
I feel u penetrating me mentally...
I sit in remembrance of the exposure of your lips
Softly, gently your hands upon my hips...
Do u remember?
Warm days with the sun shining bright
Thinkin' lovely thoughts well into the night
Am I wrong or right?
Constantly your arms embrace all contents of me, but u are no longer with me
How can this b
That your eyes are all I c?
As I think of u, r u thinkin' bout me?

Have You?

Have you ever felt a feeling?
I mean, really felt a feeling that taps into your being?
Something so strong, so magnetic,
That at times it's hard to believe what you are seeing?

Have you ever had a kiss?
No not just a kiss, but a physical attachment, emotional link?
When their face appears with each free moment,
Their presence is there, when they are not, each thought that you think…

Have you ever loved a love?
More than just the idea of it, but a penetration of the soul?
Caring, concern, yearning, longing for their presence,
A love that you know can make you again completely whole?

Have you ever been tempted?
I mean, not just a notion to act, but almost like being led to do it?
Throwing all inhibitions to the wind and to live for the moment,
And only for the moment, no longer pushing to the limits, go through with it?

Have you ever known that a situation should have never occurred?
Maybe longing for that one touch, or thought, or feeling; make it take place?
To learn from love, to learn what love would be like if it thrived off of every word…
Or to leave it alone as it is, and wipe it clean as though it never left a trace.

Have you ever learned to let go?
I mean really, really let go, when you want to hold tight?
Walking away when you don't want to, when that love won't grow?
But you have to let go, because it was never right...

Realization

Tears fall from her eyes in silent huddled masses; she wondered what it was that she did wrong.
She was faithful, loving; how could something become so weak, that was once so strong?
She loved him with everything; heart, body, soul and mind Nevertheless, peace of mind he took from her, and that again she will never find.
Why couldn't it be as if it was in the fairytales, where only people had fear of falling?
Now her tears have fears too, and her lonely heart is calling
As the tears silently fall, they leave a message: the drip drop and pitter-patter on the ground
Equivalent to her heart's lonely sound -
How could she make it better? She did not know what to do; what to say -
All she could do was wish in her heart, but never ask, hoping he would stay
Never did she know that she did not lose anything until she said that all was lost -
Moreover, as always in love, her heart was the cost . . .

Night Sky

Comets light the cool night sky
As explosions of hopes and dreams fade with you and I
Cry?
Never.
The crying of my heart calms the night's weather.
A cool chill brushes my cheek as I recall all the dreams we had in common
All of the dreams we have-had not now, but then
You possess a part of my being that no one else could touch
I gave you all of me, because you loved me just as much
I bared my soul to you.
Gave you the center of my universe with a ring on your finger
Unfortunate memories of your scent still lingers
Danger overshadowed my heart as I submerged into your eyes...
Everyone told me that this union was wrong, but I was convinced they were lies
Secret life, secret identity, secret all that ever existed
How could I have been such a fool that it walked right past, and I missed it?
Twisted
Thoughts break free from an imprisoned mind and torment my ears
But everything that I once heard has become my most anguished fears
Dismembered hopes
Living lies and jokes

Emma Joan

Emotions completely broke . . .
And in the sky the stars form an almost inevitable shape...
As I, on my own, try to outrun fate . . .

I Am...

I am the dust that rises and settles with heaven's every breath
I am that 12th rib, man's completion; his protection...
I am selected to give birth to nations; this body houses future kings, queens and leaders
I am the essence of life...

I am that ingenious student at the top of her class
I am that dedicated careerist taking care of home and employees
I am that mother, that father, that wife, that sister, that daughter, holding everything together in perfect harmony
I am God's truest demonstration of strength...

I am not stuck on myself; my giving nature to nurture makes me who I am - what I am
I am not a just a pretty face, a size, a prize or an arm piece
My intellect is deeply rooted in Rome, my artistry built its foundation
I am truly a lady as intended...

I am to be placed on a pedestal, waited on hand and foot; embraced
I am every race, every shape, every creed and every color
I am everything that I was made to be
I am WOMAN...

I'll Never Stop

I'll never stop loving you, no matter what the day
Even now, I wonder why someone so precious had to go away
So young, so full of potential the best at whatever you do;
If anyone had my heart, though I was young, it had to be you...

I'll never stop playing those songs we used to sing...
Or reading about mythical dragons, and little girls bearing wings
Or writing poems of love and romance
Or teaching all of our friends that love would soon entrance

I'll never stop reminiscing on all of the times that we shared
Or how many arguments we had, then told each other how much we cared
It need not be said that we were closer than friends
We were family, and no matter what happened, you and I both knew our love would never end...

I'll never stop reminding myself of how good of a team we made
Nor of all the soul redemption rules we laid
I can't possibly ponder all of the things that you are doing now
But surely, whatever it is you are doing it in style

I'll never stop knowing that you are beautiful and kind
My inspiration, forever alive in my mind
I'll never stop remembering to keep your memory up to par
I can't wait to see you again one day, my true shining star

I'll never stop . . .

Had It Been . . .

Why should I, why have I, why am I spending my time
Or have I always been, and still forever am, living for a love that wasn't mine?
Have I made mistakes I would have never made, had life always been fair?
Would I have suffered the same pain, loved the same way, if you were never there?

Could I have opened my heart without a single thought, if I knew you didn't care?
Yes indeed, I thought, and with my mind I fought, because you were always there
But I brought this on, did I not? I think so.
But had the tables flipped, I still would have slipped deep in, and not have let you go.

But should I have? (I have) and I should have laughed (I have) at the thought of letting you stay
Then I realize, I am the prize—and I am so glad to send you on your way . . .

What About...

I try to block out all of the times you hurt me and I hurt you All the times we denied our love and we both knew it was true The love we had was completely original, untainted and so pure, We were together forever, for life, of that I was sure -
Now we hardly even talk and you never communicate with me; Tell me, really, is this the way a relationship should be?
I remember we—you used to love me like no other
And we sat for hours at a time and we held each other
There was no separating us, the bond between us was so tight;
And whenever we were not together, something wasn't right...
What about now, it seems that the less we see of each other, the better off we are
You are standing right in front of me, yet you seem so far
I wish I could understand you, just have an inkling of what is on your mind;
I wish I knew what you needed to find.
What about the times we made each other cry in vain?
The way we caused each other all of this unnecessary pain?
How could we do this to each other and call what we have love?

A Story

Resilient and bold… never ceases to amaze
Strong in our ways
But can the prize be found at the end of the maze?

Thoughts untold, too much for the human mind to behold
With words, words that shape create and mold;
So long is the story untold…

Conscious in thought, so long we've toiled and fought
Still with a price our lives were bought;
The fateful answer to why is still sought -

Black, bold and beautiful, black, bold and proud
Can be spotted anywhere in a crowd.
Our actions aren't mild.
Can't shut up we've done that for too long; You hear one voice clear, free and loud;

Freedom of speech- they shouldn't have let us have that one for fun
So before it's all said and done
Unified we stand under the sun
The dust rises and settles and an army we have become

Waiting . . . prepared . . . as one . . ..

I'm Not The Redeemer

While these cats are drownin', I got the lifeboat
Searchin' for new hopes
Holdin' on to life like a handle
Steady burnin' down is my candle

Evolution screams for appeasement- The very reason I was sent
So concerned about what you think is poppin'
Never stopping'
To ask questions
Second guessin'
Everything

They call me Preach and say I teach the masses
How to bring dark hopes from the vastness
But who brings my velvet rope of hope?
Sure enough I rescue these drownin' cats from the raging rivers of time,
But really am I committing a crime?

Whoever said I had to save the multitude from their sins? When true salvation is within
Yourself
Makin' it seem like I'm the light in this would of dark
My soul embarks on a journey where I should have learned
Strengthened bridges I've burned

Feelin' like the Anti-Christ because everyone follows my lead
It's hard not to lose self

To the wealth of these sinners I'm supposed to be savin'
Tryin' not to lose self and prepare everyone for the last days
Pleadin' with God so I can see the pearly gates
No one can relate
I sit sedated from a drug that takes soul possession
I should be confessin'
But I gotta rescue you from drownin'.
I would say get in my lifeboat
And search for new hopes
With me

But I don't know where my search will lead me to be
The salvation I am thought to possess is the very salvation I need;
I dig the fact that the world is full of dreamers
But they gotta realize I'm NOT THE REDEEMER . . .

Whatever You Want It To Be

Catastrophic interruptions in life's balance
Undeniable forces pose a threat - if you will a challenge.
Multiple problems penetrate my living spot
Bringing to me issues that I have long since forgot
Bringing me drama, right when it's hot
Making me cold when inside- I'm not...
Fingers and gats pop
I'm still waiting for my audience to transcend and the non-sense to stop
Listening to myself read,
Internally I bleed
From a shattered glass heart's fractured existence...
I lift my arms for hope from a foreign resistance
I miss this...
That one moment before time
When life flowed in continuous rhyme
But now, now no one seems to care
I see your eyes concentrating, but are you still there?
I think that this mental eclipse has opened my eyes to see,
It's not reality, but whatever you want it to be . . .

Still Searchin'

I found out a lot of things that I did not know,
I've turned in so many directions when
everyone and everything said no
I had to learn for myself.
Working hard on this writing thing, 'cause
my spirit it could always lift
Most say I'm not using it properly 'cause it's a God-given gift
I hear 'em talkin' but I don't pay 'em no mind
None of them choose or walk my roads
for me—the WAY I gotta find
My thoughts get a little blurry as I write "Beginner's Mind"
At the end of the book, and my way I still can't find
But my knowledge will begin to show
Everything that I think I know . . .
I wonder if when I speak, the outside world
can tell that I am still workin'
'Cause the truth of the matter is, no matter what I find, I'm still
searchin' . . .

www.ingramcontent.com/pod-product-compliance
Lightning Source LLC
LaVergne TN
LVHW011727060526
838200LV00051B/3052